Blank Canvas

Blank Canvas
Published by Cyan Tayse
Copyright © 2017 Cyan Tayse

Licence Notes

Proofreading and Editing by Spell Bound
Cover images from Pixabay

ISBN: 978-0-473-40896-1
ISBN: 978-0-473-40897-8

Other books by Cyan Tayse

Pocket Rocket Novellas
(A series of standalone shorts)

Have you Ever...?
Blank Canvas

Blank Canvas
A Pocket Rocket Novella

By Cyan Tayse

Chapter one

Hailee

"No, no, no, no, no!" I run down the corridor, my eyes searching for the right room, as my sweater, which is tied loosely around my waist, slowly begins to unravel and slip down my hips. Shoving my paint brush into my mouth, and balancing everything else against my hip, I grab both sleeves and give a sharp yank, pulling it as tight as I can.

"Room 107, room 107," I chant as I run past each door. My first ever Life Drawing class and I'm running late. Not exactly a good start to the semester. In my defence though, my trusty Toyota Starlet had decided that today was the day it was going to give up the ghost and conk out on the side of the road about ten blocks from here. Lugging a box of charcoals, a sketch pad and a set of acrylic paints in my arms while I frantically ran the half marathon to get here, was no easy feat.

Perhaps I've brought too many supplies for my first day, but I like to be prepared. The class description had been rather vague, stating only that we would "learn new techniques and unleash our inner artist". Considering the funk I've been in over the last few months, I'm willing to give anything a crack.

My creative juices had up and left me around the same time my girlfriend, Lila, had up and left in the middle of the night, along with the fortnight's rent money, my favourite pair of shoes, and for some reason unknown to me, my unfinished tribute to the Christchurch Cathedral – a modern replica made entirely of carved Oamaru Stone, complete with stained-glass windows. I had spent days preparing the individual blocks and assembling them, having only completed three walls before it had disappeared. Every window had been welded into an arc before colourful beads of plastic had been arranged inside the frames and baked to achieve the stained-glass look. I'd been working on it for a month, hoping to donate it to the Museum's display on Christchurch post-quake.

That dream went flying out the window along with any other aspirations I had as soon as I woke up to an empty home and an irate landlord pounding on my door.

Art is all I know. It's all I've ever wanted to do, and I'm good at it. A natural, some might say. I can find the beauty in almost anything and make a small living by sketching caricatures of passing tourists, finding their best feature and making it shine.

I love to experiment with all different types of artwork; building models, sketching, photography, jewellery. You name it, I've tried it. But my real passion, the one I want to really perfect, is painting. I've spent many hours wandering the halls of the Art Gallery, paying close attention to every brush stroke, every colour blend. One day I want to have my paintings on those very walls. To inspire a budding artist just like me. To be the next Leonardo DaVinci, Picasso, or Michelangelo.

Which is why, after a swift kick in the ass by my bestie, I enrolled in this class. If I am going to become a household name, I need to knuckle down and hone my skills.

I try to remind myself of this as I race down the corridors, finally stumbling into room 107, and straight into the back of an older gentleman draped in a satin robe with his walking socks pulled up to his knees.

"Excuse me, I'm s-so sorry," I stutter, dropping to the floor to collect my scattered belongings.

"You must be Hailee?" A slender pair of legs stand in front of me, a hand proffered for me to accept.

Gathering everything against my chest, I grip her slight hand, giving a gentle squeeze as

I nod my head. "Y-yes, that's me. I'm sorry I'm late. My car broke down."

"These things happen. We're just about to get started. Would you like to take the easel over here?" She waves her hand out to the side where the remaining unclaimed easel stands, patiently waiting. "You can put your effects on the shelf below. We'll be starting with some warm-up sketches." Moving back to the front of the class, she clasps her hands in front of her, waiting for me to get set up. "For those of you who are new to this class, my name is Angelique, and I will endeavour to take you on a journey of creativity. I want to expand your minds and take you out of your comfort zones." Smoothing her wispy hair behind her ear, she continues, slowly walking around the room. "Face your easels, close your eyes and take a deep, cleansing breath. Now, open your eyes and begin."

Chapter Two

Aroha

Sweat drips from my brow as I move my feet to the beat in time with the instructor.

"And squeeeeeeze! Come on, ladies!" If she squeezes any harder, she is going to give herself a hernia. Her eyes are bugging out and her face is bright red. It makes me glad there aren't any mirrors in here. If the instructor, an ex-runway model, looks like that, I hate to think what my face looks like after twenty minutes of intense step aerobics.

Glancing to my left, I see that Sophia is bouncing around the floor like a graceful gazelle. Ever the beauty queen, that one. She'd convinced me to come along and try out her gym—it may have had something to do with her lycra leotard—and somehow, I ended up signing up for step class.

I've always prided myself in being relatively fit and healthy, but the whole dance-your-way-to-fitness fad has never really appealed to me in the slightest. All it had taken was one glance at Sophia's supple thighs in her skin-tight get-up, to convince me otherwise.

Of course, once class actually started, I quickly regretted my decision. Grace and timing have never been strengths of mine. I'm more of a run-in-short-bursts type of girl. None of this hour-long prancing around business.

Halfway through and I can barely catch my breath, let alone co-ordinate my feet to step one in front of the other. That will teach me for following Sophia around like a horn dog. I know she's straight and in love with her boyfriend of three years, but that doesn't mean I can't look. You've gotta have goals in life, and finding someone like her is my goal. I like to think of her as a real-life vision board. If you see it, it will eventually become your reality.

"And luuuuuuunge! Drop it low, ladies!" the instructor bellows and I'm forced to pay attention again. Widening my stance, I attempt to follow along in time to the music, but my muscles are seizing and I can't get back out of the godforsaken pose.

"What are you doing, Aroha?" Sophia giggles as she lunges in perfect synchronicity with the rest of the class. Once again reminding me how out of my depth I am.

"Just, ah, taking a breather." I circle my arms in an arc toward the ground then reach up to the ceiling like Suzy Aitken in the *Fit Kit*, taking a deep breath and puffing it out. I don't know how much longer I can fake being okay with this. My thighs are burning and streams of sweat pour down the sides of my face as my whole body begins to shudder.

"Are you okay?" she asks, a look of worry marring her beautiful features. She stops lunging and stares at me with a cocked head.

"Mmhmm," I hum through pursed lips. *Come on, legs! Don't fail me now!*

"You don't look so good." She steps in closer, her eyes squinting while she assesses me. "Are you… stuck?" The amusement in her eyes doesn't go unnoticed.

"I may… be having… a little… difficulty… getting out of this… hold." I force the words through clenched teeth as I try to blink the sweat away from my eyes. My thighs shudder beneath me and a gasp falls from my lips. "Oh shit!" And like a slow-motion movie, my legs buckle and I begin my clumsy descent to the floor.

Sophia rushes over to me, quite obviously trying not to laugh at my expense. "Are you okay?" she manages to say before sucking her lips in to stop them from lifting into a smile.

Not wanting any more attention drawn my way, I wave her off. "Don't mind me, I'm good. As you were." With a shrug of her shoulders, she steps back into line and picks up where she left off.

I sit, staring at my traitorous legs, wishing the ground would swallow me up. My only saving grace at this point, is that the door is just to my left. Doing a bum-shuffle, I slip to the back of the class and on shaky legs, I pick myself up off the floor and make a beeline for the door.

Blank Canvas

Chapter Three

Hailee

Holding my pencil out in front of me, I squint one eye, trying to get an idea of proportions. Alfred, the older gentleman I collided with earlier, is perched on a wooden rocking chair, sans robe, one leg crossed over the other and a smoking pipe held between his lips. He still wears his knee-length walking socks and sandals, but that is the extent of his coverings.

I knew there would be nude models for us to draw, I just hadn't expected... well... this. To say I'm a little uncomfortable sketching a naked old man is an understatement, but, I pull up my big girl panties and try to ignore the fact that there appears to be a wiry hairball sitting in his lap.

It's for the greater good, I tell myself. *Before you can fly, you must learn to walk.* Or in this case, before I can paint the intricacies needed for beautifully detailed portraits, I must first learn how to sketch and shade the nooks and crevices of this weathered man and his precariously perched parts.

"Ah, yes. You have a good eye, I see." Angelique smiles at me, her delicate fingers coming to rest on my shoulders. "Remember, though, this is just a warm-up exercise. Rather than sketching the muse in his entirety, focus on one aspect and highlight it." She snags a charcoal pencil from behind her ear, and on a fresh sheet of paper, she begins to draw feathered lines. Her eyes dart up to the front of the class and back to the paper continuously, her hand never leaving the page. Within a matter of minutes, an image forms of just his hand reaching for the pipe.

"Wow, that's beautiful," I say under my breath.

"When you focus on just one element, you allow your eyes to pick up so much more detail." She tucks her pencil back behind her ear. "Give it a go. See what you can come up with."

Just one element. I can do this.

Taking hold of my pencil, I rest my hand against the paper and turn my eyes back to Alfred. Following her lead, my hand dusts across the page, as I focus solely on his ankle and foot. I try to capture the bunched sock where his sandal begins, the curve of his flexed toe. Everything else fades into a blur around me and I can almost see each individual strand of woven thread as I relax my eyes.

It's not until Alfred changes position that I finally blink and sit back, peering at my page. *Not bad.*

"New sheet of paper, and back into it," Angelique says from somewhere across the room. "This time, pay attention to where the light is coming in to the room, where it's landing on Alfred. Really exaggerate the shadows and highlights, without neglecting the true form."

Tilting my head side-to-side, I stare at the sheet of paper blankly. It's impossibly warm in here and I'm finding it hard to concentrate. Shucking the sweater from my hips and rolling up my sleeves, I huff out a breath and close my eyes. With my pencil at the ready, I open my eyes, stepping forward. Zeroing in on the angle of his shoulders, and the way he holds his head just so, my hand flies across the paper, trying to capture his very essence.

Once I'm satisfied with the shapes, I switch to a heavier charcoal and work on the shading around his neck. My thumb drags along the page, smudging the sharp black edges, giving them a softer appearance. I work my way up, adding a light dusting of stubble along his jaw, and accentuating the hook of his nose.

His deep-set eyes look off into space, his brow furrowed, and I'm curious as to what he's thinking. It takes some guts to strip yourself bare in front of a group of strangers, scrutinising your body for the sake of art. I guess I can see how it could be quite freeing though, shedding the shackles that society places on us all and embracing the beauty of your own body. Not giving a damn what anyone thinks. And really, why *should* he care what others think? The human body is fascinating and beautiful. It carries us where we need to go, has the power to create life, and gives us the tools we need to build and grow. No two bodies are the same, and that, in itself, is amazing. It's one of the reasons why I wanted to do this class. To be able to replicate that beauty that resides in all of us, and showcase the differences and similarities we each hold. To find that light, and let it shine.

Perhaps in doing so, I could find the light that's been missing from mine too.

Chapter Four

Aroha

"It's not that bad," Sophia says, securing her towel around her body.

"Easy for you to say, you're not the one who collapsed in the middle of a step class." I gather my things, trying not to let my eyes linger on her curves. Knowing she is naked beneath that towel is doing my head in.

"I don't think anyone noticed. You'll get it next time, don't worry."

"Oh no." I hold my hand up to stop her. "There won't be a next time. Once was more than enough for me."

"Oh, come on, you can't give up after one class!" She puts her hands on her hips in a no-nonsense kind of way.

"I most certainly can, and I most certainly will." I fold my arms across my chest defiantly. "You'll have to find yourself another step buddy. Sorry." I let my eyes travel the length of her body before turning back to my bag. "I'll wait out in the foyer while you get dressed."

Without waiting for a response, I power walk out the door, needing to put some distance between us. It's impossible to keep my mind out of the gutter when she's standing mere inches away in next to nothing. It's moments like these I thank my lucky stars that I'm not a man, because I would be sporting some serious wood right now.

At least the foyer offers some relief. The air is cooler out here and helps clear my mind. I don't know what I was thinking coming here.

Knowing I can never have her, but putting myself through the sweet torture of watching her bend and twist her lithe body in that 'leaving-nothing-to-the-imagination' leotard was a stupid mistake.

I need to get my head out of the clouds, find something else to occupy my time. Sophia will never be mine, I know that, and unless I put myself out there, I'm never going to find what I'm looking for.

With renewed purpose, I push my shoulders back and march to the noticeboard. Perhaps there is a class I can take, something that will broaden my horizons.

The board is filled with posters about body health, personal trainers and health supplements, but one small notice, tucked in behind, piques my interest.

NUDE MODELS WANTED

Models of any shape, size and ethnicity wanted for Life Drawing Class. No experience necessary.

Must be over 18

If interested, please phone Angelique on 03 3885 968

Nude modelling. If anything is going to broaden my horizons and get me out of my comfort zone, that would be it. But, could I do it? Could I actually strip down in front of complete strangers?

Before I even know what I'm doing, my phone is in my hand, snapping a picture of the flyer for future reference. I guess it couldn't hurt to look into it further.

"You ready to go?" Sophia latches onto my arm, making me jump. "Ooh, what's got you all riled up?" She chuckles, looking up to the board that has held my attention for the past few minutes. With a click of her tongue, she points at the very notice I've been staring at. "Can you believe that? Who in their right mind would volunteer for that?" She shudders. "All those random people staring at you… makes my skin crawl."

Instantly on the defensive, I raise an eyebrow at her. "Really? That's a little close-minded, don't you think? It's not like it's a room full of perverts. It's art."

"You're not…" She flicks her finger back and forth between me and the board. "You're not actually considering this, are you?"

"What if I am?" I pull my arm out from her grasp. "I think it could be interesting."

"Or dangerous. Why would you put yourself in such a vulnerable position?" She scrunches her nose at me.

"I don't know, maybe to put myself out there. Try something different. It's not like I have anything else going on right now."

"Aren't you worried what they'll draw? What if it's not… flattering?" Her eyes flit up and down my body, landing on the ink peeking out of my top.

"Why wouldn't it be flattering?" I cock my hip, interested to hear what she has to say.

She coughs, shuffling her feet. "You know, you've got all those tattoos… it might not be easy…"

"You don't like my tattoos?"

"No! *I* like them, but, you know, they're not for everyone."

Huh. You think you know someone…

"Well, it's a good thing I don't get them to please anyone else then, eh?" I swing my bag over my shoulder and walk towards the door. "And if they don't like them, then so be it. I'm not embarrassed by who I am or how I look."

"So, you're going to do it then?" she asks with a look of complete and utter horror.

I stop walking and look at her. Up until this very moment, I hadn't decided either way, but something in her words makes me want to prove a point. I *am* proud of this body, tattoos and all. "Yeah, I guess I am."

Chapter Five

Hailee

Throwing my things on the table, I put the kettle on the stove on the way past before flopping down onto the couch. It's been a long day. After spending an entire afternoon at the studio, I then had to trudge back to my car and call a mechanic to get towed. I'd had to wait over an hour for someone to show up and even though the sky was beginning to darken, the guy refused to give me a lift, saying something about company policy. So, once my car was securely locked away in their garage for the night, I began the trek back home, juggling my art supplies once again, and dreaming of a hot cup of tea and a soak in the tub.

"It's not going to run itself," I say out loud, pushing up from the couch. The bathroom is small and dank, but I make the most of the space I've got, lighting the candles that line the windowsill and bath. There's something so calming about a flickering flame that sets my mind at ease.

With the taps on full, I step out of the room to finish making my cup of tea before grabbing my dog-eared copy of *Much Ado About Nothing*. I've read it so many times over the years, I've lost count. It's my go-to book for whenever I need a pick-me-up. The witty banter between Benedick and Beatrice somehow always manages to make a bad day good. And today is certainly a day when I need that.

Positioning the little table within arm's reach of the bath, I place my tea and book on top, a washcloth beside them for drying my hands. Slowly pulling my arms from my sleeves and stepping out of my jeans, I take a weary breath. Tomorrow will be a better day, I can feel it.

I test the water with my toes before slipping under, instantly feeling the burdens of the day washing away. I let my mind wander back to the studio, picturing myself standing in front of the room wearing only a robe and a smile. I move to the chaise set on a raised platform, seductively letting the robe slip from my shoulders. Reaching up, I pull the pin from my hair, letting it cascade down my back in soft waves. A nervous hum slips from my mouth as my bare skin slides along the silky fabric of the chaise. A tingle of excitement runs down my spine and hardens my nipples as I turn my gaze on the class before me. This is it, I'm exposed in the most intimate of ways, and it's both exhilarating and excruciating. My heart feels as though it may beat out of my chest as my eyes travel around the room, watching the interest of my peers as they take in my vulnerability.

Opening my eyes, I am surprised to find myself somewhat aroused by that little imagining. My fingers trail delicately down my body to the vee between my thighs. I rest my head back as I sink lower into the water, my fingers lazily circling my clit, stirring up a dormant heat inside.

Cupping my breast, I pinch the tightened bud between my finger and thumb. My hips buck at the sensation coursing through my body, and my finger picks up the pace. I bite my lip and close my eyes, picturing my naked body on display once more.

My hand slides down my torso, finding the place I need it the most. Gently running my fingers along the cleft where my thighs meet my most sensitive part, I hold my breath as I plunge inside. A sigh escapes my lips as I move my fingers languidly in and out, the intensity building.

I slip a second finger in, pressing firmer against my nub as my hips rock back and forth. "God," I hiss under my breath as I reach the precipice of my desire. My walls pulse against my fingers as they draw out their sweet torment.

My ragged breath stills and I'm left staring at the ceiling in surprise. It's been a while since I've succumbed to the indulgence of pleasure; even at my own hands.

With a smile on my face, I sink further into the water, taking a moment to enjoy the quiet calm that has enveloped me.

Chapter Six

Aroha

"Thank you so much for contacting me." Angelique beams and ushers me into her office. "It takes a special kind of person willing to do this, and volunteers are few and far between as you can probably imagine." She directs me to a worn couch with a crochet throw draped over top.

"To be honest, I wasn't even sure I'd make it here. I've never done anything like this before." I settle on the edge of the couch, ready for a quick getaway if necessary. "What exactly would I have to do?"

"There's really nothing set in concrete. I like my models to be comfortable and choose their own poses and props. What my students are learning is how to define the body and turn it into a work of art. Every body is different, so it's nice for them to have various models to work with." She perches on the corner of her desk, crossing her feet in front of her. "As the ad said, I'm looking for people who are comfortable in their own skin, enough to go sans clothes. Of course, with this being your first time, we can always have you draped in a robe until you're more comfortable if you'd like." She smiles warmly, putting me at ease.

"I could really do that? Wear a robe?"

"Sure. It's all about the shapes and shades after all." She stands, grabbing a discarded shawl and wrapping it around her shoulders. "A robe would add another dimension, a new texture."

Her smile is contagious. "Well, it sounds easy enough."

"It is. I think you'll be surprised. You might even enjoy it."

I chuckle, pushing myself up off the couch. "I don't know if I'd go that far, but I'll give it a crack. If you want me, that is." My top lifts, exposing my stomach as I rub my hand along the back of my neck. Her eyes travel down to my bare skin, taking in the ink on display.

"You have some artwork of your own I see."

"Uh, yeah. Is that going to be okay?"

She brushes her hair behind her ear, as she glides across the room, placing her hands on my shoulders. "This is a Life Drawing class. *Life.* We accept any and all bodies in here. No discrimination." Her hands slide down my arms to give a gentle squeeze before she leads me towards the door. "It will give them a nice challenge too." She winks.

"Oh, well, okay then." I muster a smile. "Well, when would you like me to start?"

"As luck would have it, I have an opening this afternoon if you're free."

"Oh, wow, that soon?"

"Yes, I'm afraid my other model called in sick today, so this is perfect timing." She opens the door, resting her arm against it. "I understand if it's too soon."

"No, no. I don't have any plans, so I may as well jump straight in before I get cold feet!" I laugh nervously.

"You're a Godsend," Angelique gushes. "Thank you so much. Class starts at 3pm, so if you want to get here about quarter of an hour beforehand to get ready, then I can show you what to do."

"Sounds like a plan, Stan." I have a tendency to make up silly rhymes to amuse myself when I'm nervous, so when the words slip from my mouth, I cringe. Clearing my throat, I step out the door and wave. "See you this afternoon!"

Chapter Seven

Hailee

Heat rushes to my cheeks as the class comes into view. My little daydream had kept me awake most of the night, unable to shake the feeling of all those eyes devouring my naked body. I never imagined such a thing could turn me on so much, but here I am, art supplies clutched in my hands as my centre pulses between my thighs.

Forcing my legs to move, I reach out, my hand hovering over the handle as I try to steady my breath.

"Are you, um, modelling too?" a voice speaks up from behind me and I squeal in surprise. "Shit, sorry. I didn't mean to scare you."

"It's okay," I say with a giggle, turning my back to the door and coming face to face with the black-haired beauty. Her emerald coloured eyes stare back at me with amusement.

"Ah, you're a student." She nods at my armload of supplies, pulling the corner of her plump lip between her teeth.

"I am. You're modelling for us today?" I ask nervously. Something about the way this girl with skin like chocolate is watching me, has my heart racing.

"If I can get over my nerves." She grins, shifting the bag on her shoulder. "I've never done this before, and I wasn't expecting anyone my age to be here." She shakes her head with a laugh. "Silly, isn't it? I don't know why I thought that."

"It's okay. You can just picture me naked."
What??

"Um…"

"Um… I mean, ya know, because that's what they tell you to do when you're nervous, isn't it?" *Kill me, kill me now.*

"I'm getting my kit off, not public speaking. But thanks, I just might do that." Her eyes sparkle as she teases, and I can't help but grin back at her.

We both go to move at the same time, ending up in a dance of sorts as we try to manoeuvre through the door.

"Ah, Aroha, you made it," Angelique says from the front of the class. "I was beginning to worry you'd changed your mind."

"I was this close," she holds up her finger and thumb to demonstrate, "but the lovely…" she turns to face me with a quirk of her brow.

"Hailee."

"Hailee." The word seems to roll off her tongue as if it belongs there. "The lovely Hailee gave me some good advice." She throws me a wink and then follows Angelique through to her office.

I take advantage of the empty class and select an easel in the centre, giving me a better view of the platform she'll be on. My heart pitter-patters at the thought of seeing her disrobed. I know it's wrong. I'm here to learn, not ogle. But the girl with ebony hair has somehow got under my skin.

Chapter Eight

Aroha

"How do you feel?" Angelique asks as I step out from behind the curtain, my fingers clutching the robe in place in front of me. It's an odd feeling to be standing in a room with a woman I've only just met, knowing I'm completely naked beneath this thin layer of satin.

"Um, okay I guess." I shrug my shoulders, swallowing the lump that has settled in my throat. *You can do this. It's only skin.*

She smiles at me, making me feel a little less vulnerable. "Stay in here a few more minutes, get used to the idea. I'll go through and get them started on a warm-up until you're ready."

"Okay." I nod, moving over to the couch in the corner, suddenly realising I have no clue what I'm meant to do. "Wait!" She quirks a brow at me. "Um, how do I do this? I mean, do I just strut out there in my birthday suit and strike a pose?"

She laughs, sweeping a hand over her hair. "If that's what you want to do, it's fine by me, but most people tend to wear the robe until they're in place and ready to begin."

"Oh, right. Yeah, that makes sense."

She pushes through the door and I'm left standing here with my nerves slowly getting the better of me. I pace back and forth in front of the couch, chewing my thumbnail, wondering how long I should wait.

"Screw it." I march over to the door and peer through the tiny sliver of a window. Everyone has their eyes directed at their easels, their hands already moving across the page. My eyes land on Hailee, sitting front and centre, her blonde hair swept into a messy bun on the top of her head. One strap of her oversized singlet hangs loosely from her arm, as she cocks her head and moves to smudge the charcoal on the page. She looks as though she belongs in this world.

I step back from the door and run a hand around to the back of my neck. This is it. Show time.

Pushing on the door, I slip silently into the room. The wooden floor is cold beneath my feet, but the room itself is almost tropical.

To my right is an old rocking chair and side table, to my left, a velvety chaise lounge, similar to what you'd see in a Victorian movie. Its burgundy fabric looks worn but cosy, and I'm drawn to it.

No one seems to have noticed me enter the room. No one, except Hailee. Her grey-blue eyes hold mine, a hint of a smile on her lips. I can't seem to look away, almost as if we're locked in a staring contest.

When my fingers graze the edge of the chaise, my gaze falters, and I turn briefly to look at the piece of furniture. When my eyes flick back up to hers, it's as though a fire has ignited in them. She fiddles with her pencil, her teeth gnawing at her bottom lip as she watches me lower myself down to the cushion.

"Are you almost ready?" Angelique's smiling face appears in front of me, and I blink to clear my eyes.

"Mmhmm." I stroke the fabric beside me. "Do I just… strip?"

"If you feel comfortable doing so. Otherwise, in the robe is fine." She stepped back, addressing the class. "Right. We have a new model for you today. She's just getting set up and then we can begin. We'll keep it to the charcoal for now, and move onto paint tomorrow if you feel like you're ready for it."

Taking a deep breath, I slide my body down the length of the chaise, my eyes searching out Hailee once more. I'm like an addict, I can't get enough of those eyes and the way they watch me.

Licking my lips, I turn my body slightly, bending one arm behind my head, while the other slides down my side. Her eyes follow my hand, and when I reach around to the front of the robe, pulling it open slightly, her pupils dilate and her mouth drops open in a tiny gasp. There's something very erotic in the way she's watching me, like she's mesmerised by me. It helps me to forget the many sets of eyes on me at this very moment.

She takes her time, those grey-blue orbs trailing slowly back up the length of my body, lingering on the swell of my breasts, before meeting my eyes again. A gentle blush colours her cheeks as she gives me a shy smile before turning her attention to the page in front of her.

Chapter Nine

Hailee

It's as if my dream is playing out before my very eyes, only this time instead of me being the centre of everyone's attention, it's Aroha. My mind brings back the feelings of unbridled arousal I'd felt, sending a warmth pulsing through my body and settling in the apex of my thighs.

She really is exquisite.

My pencil finds a steady rhythm, caressing the page with strokes ever so gentle as I try to capture her beauty. The robe leaves a lot to the imagination, giving us only a glimpse, but somehow that seems more intimate.

Peeking out from beneath the silky fabric covering her breast is the beginnings of a tribal tattoo. My mind goes into overdrive as I wonder how far across it reaches, how detailed it is. I find myself staring, willing the robe to move and expose just a little bit more.

As if she can read my mind, she arches her back just a touch, her eyes locked on mine. I'm given a peek at just a bit more skin, the ink weaving a tale of its own as it darts under the fabric around her neck.

"Yes, I love what you've done here." Angelique appears beside me, jolting me from my thoughts. A blush heats my cheeks as I turn my gaze to her, hoping she can't tell how affected I am by our latest model. "Very detailed. You've captured her expression well." With a pat of my shoulder, she moves on to the next student, barely batting an eye. I huff out the breath I've been holding, squeezing my eyes shut as I rub my fingertips across my temple.

What am I doing? Fantasising over this girl I've barely even met, that's what I'm doing. Trying not to get caught watching her, that's what I'm doing. Trying not to imagine what it would be like to see her without her robe, baring her soul to only me.

I shake my head, admonishing myself. This isn't me, this isn't who I am. I'm not some sex-crazed hussy, I'm an artist. I'm here to learn not find a hook-up.

I let my mind wander to the one person it shouldn't. Lila. She nearly destroyed me when she left. I barely ate or slept, and my art went by the wayside. I won't let that happen again. I can't.

Lifting my eyes to the paper in front of me, I scrutinise my work. Angelique is right, I *have* captured her expression well. The full pout of her lips, the way her eyes look as though they see through to my very core. She's mesmerising. So much so, my thoughts of Lila disappear.

I find myself stealing a look out the corner of my eye, and instantly, Aroha meets my gaze, the hint of a smirk gracing her lips as if she really *can* read my mind. I feel that blush deepen, but no matter how hard I try, I can't turn away. I'm hypnotised by the brilliant tones of her eyes.

Chapter Ten

Aroha

With a grin plastered on my face, I walk out to my car, throwing my bag in the backseat. I'm still buzzing from the excitement of it all. I don't know why more people don't do nude modelling, it's so… exhilarating. Like the high I imagine actor's get when they're up on stage performing in front of a live audience. There's nothing quite like it, knowing that all eyes are on you.

The one downfall is that Hailee disappeared in a flash once class was over. I was hoping to ask her if she wanted to go for a coffee or something. I'm sure I hadn't imagined the attraction between us, but she didn't even stick around long enough for me to throw some clothes on. She just up and left.

Oh well, I'm sure I'll see her again at the next class. Angelique said she was always on the lookout for more models, and I could do with the cash. May as well kill two birds with one stone.

I climb into the driver's seat and wind the window down, letting the cool air blow across my face. While the car warms up, I select a CD at random, firing it in and cranking up the sound. The unmistakeable sound of piano keys and Bonnie Tyler singing *Total Eclipse of the Heart* rings through the car, and without missing a beat, I jump in, singing at full volume. Nothing like a good power ballad singalong while you're driving home.

I pull out of the carpark and head down the road, singing my little heart out. I even do a bit of shoulder dancing, swinging my head side-to-side.

In the middle of belting out the chorus, someone on the footpath catches my eye. Not just someone, but *her*.

Hailee is marching down the road with her arms full of supplies, desperately trying not to drop them. That same singlet strap has slipped once again, hindering the situation. Flicking my indicator on, I pull up beside her, winding the window down. "How much?" I ask with a grin.

She turns to me with a scowl, clearly about to give me an earful until her eyes meet mine and they light up like a Christmas tree. "Oh, hey."

"Hey yourself." I pat the seat beside me. "Hop in, I'll give you a lift."

"Oh no." She shakes her head. "I couldn't. I don't want to be a pain."

"You're not being a pain. I'm offering. And anyway," I lean across the seat, "you've seen me with my kit off. We're practically dating." I wink, pulling on the door handle.

As the door swings out, she steps out of the way, hovering on the path. Her eyes dart down the road and back to me. "Are you sure?"

"Yeah, of course. Jump in."

"Okay, thanks." She smiles and it does something to my insides. "I really appreciate it. My car broke down yesterday and it's still not fixed."

"Ugh, an extra expense you probably don't need, am I right?" I help her with her art supplies, putting them on the backseat with my bag.

"Exactly. Being an artist doesn't really pay the big bucks. Not yet anyway." She chuckles with a shrug of her shoulder. "Maybe one day."

"I'd love to see some of your work." Truth be told, I'm dying to see what she drew today. *Does that make me narcissistic?* I don't even care if it does, I want to see what she sees when she looks at me.

"Really?"

"Yeah, of course." I glance at her out the corner of my eye. "I was kinda hoping I could see what you did today." I scrunch my nose. "Is that weird? It's weird, isn't it?"

She laughs and it's like music to my ears. "No, it's not weird. I can understand wanting to see." She points up ahead. "Take the next left."

"So, you'll show me then?" I ask with a sideward glance. "What you drew today?"

"Um, yeah, sure, if you want." She plays with her fingers in her lap, looking nervous.

I reach out and touch the back of her hand, rubbing my thumb in gentle circles. "You don't have to."

She looks at my hand on hers and her blush deepens. Interesting.

After a beat, she brings her eyes up to meet mine with a small smile. "No, it's fine." She ducks her head again and looks out the window. "It's this one up here with the brown fence."

Chapter Eleven

Hailee

"You really didn't have to carry my things." I place my bag on the hook by the door, turning to grab my art supplies from her arms.

"You're not very good at accepting help, are you?" she teases. "It's really no problem."

"Well, thank you." She looks at me with a raised brow and I realise I'm being rude. I should ask her in. Stepping back, I wave a hand and usher her inside. "Uh, would you like to come in?"

"Is the sky blue?" She grins and moves past me into the cosy area I like to call my foyer, but really, it's just a glorified cloakroom about the size of a small latrine. I'd tried to spruce it up by collecting gnarled pieces of willow and adding them to a tall purple vase with realistic-looking flowers which I sat by the door. A wicker chair that I'd painted in that art deco distressed look sits proudly in the corner opposite. It's no Ritz Hotel, but it's homely, and that's what I was going for.

"Can I get you something to drink?" I skirt around her, making my way through to the kitchenette. "I've got all sorts of flavoured teas, or coffee if you'd prefer."

"Coffee would be great, thanks."

I place the kettle on the stove, turning to lean my back against the counter, my arms clasped in front of me. I take a moment to watch her as she walks around my home, her fingers trailing over some of my artworks on the wall.

"Did you do these?" she asks, her voice soft and curious as she points to the stack of canvases in the corner.

"Um, yeah." I duck my head, finding a loose thread on my top to toy with. The paintings on these walls are for everyone to see, but those ones... they're personal. They represent a time when I was broken. Not even my closest friend has seen those ones. It never occurred to me to put them away; I don't have a lot of visitors, preferring to keep to myself after Lila ran out on me. In fact, it was her leaving that spurred me to paint them. I put all my anger and hurt onto those canvases. They're nothing compared to the greats, but to me, they're beautiful.

"They're… stunning," she breaths, a hint of awe in her voice as she flicks through them, and I can't help but peek up at her. "I mean, I don't know much about art, but these… they make me *feel*, ya know?" She rests her hand across her heart, tilting her head to see them from another angle.

"Thanks. I… um… thanks."

A small chuckle rumbles through her as she turns to meet my gaze. "Not good at taking compliments either, are you?"

"I," I shake my head, giggling with her. "No, I guess not."

She moves to stand in front of me, close enough that I can smell the musky scent of her perfume. "Would you paint me?"

"I don't know… I'm still learning, that's what the class is for." I wave my hand towards the paintings in the corner. "Those were done in the heat of the moment. I took my emotions out on the canvas."

She reaches for my hand, drawing it up to rest across her heart. "Maybe," she whispers, "You could feel something else with me."

Chapter Twelve

Aroha

A bold move, I know, but there's no way I can leave here without at least trying. I know we've only just met, but Hailee is some kind of wonderful. She has a talent to be reckoned with, even if she can't see it for herself. The paintings adorning her walls are nothing short of amazing. And those ones she keeps hidden? I can feel the agony emanating from the very brush strokes, hitting like an arrow to the heart. I hope to never encounter the person who made her hurt so badly, because if I do, I don't know if I could stop myself from lashing out.

Something about this girl has every protective bone in my body on high alert, and I know I would gladly stand between her and anything that threatened to harm her.

I peer up at her, holding my breath as I wait for her answer, but her eyes stare at our hands entwined on my chest. I slide my hand down her arm, instantly missing the feel of her fingers wrapped in mine. She inhales sharply, her hand trembling as I step tentatively closer.

"Aroha." My name on her lips is the sweetest sound I've ever heard. She closes her eyes as I reach my hand up to cup her cheek. She turns into my hand, nuzzling against me, her warm breath on my skin giving me goosebumps.

I want so much to kiss her, to taste those inviting lips, but I'm scared to move too fast in case I scare her off. Instead, I settle for running the pad of my thumb along her top lip, circling down to give her bottom lip the same treatment. A soft hum slips from her mouth as she parts her lips, her tongue darting out to moisten them. The tip grazes my thumb, and I fight the urge to press inside her warmth.

The whistle of the kettle boiling jars us from our intimate moment. Hailee's eyes spring open and she takes a step back, that pink hue colouring her cheeks once more.

Clearing her throat, she turns to the stove, retrieving the steaming kettle and setting it on a holder. "How do you have your coffee?" she asks, as if we hadn't just shared something special.

"Black, no sugar. I'm sweet enough," I joke, hoping to catch a glimpse of that radiant smile again.

She nods her head in acknowledgement, pushing a cup along the bench beside her. "Here." Stepping away from me, she reaches into the fridge for the milk bottle, her hand still shaking.

"Hailee," I start, not sure what to say to put her at ease.

"It's alright." She stops me with a shake of her head. "I shouldn't have done that. That wasn't very professional." Spinning to face me, her eyes flit up to mine and back down to the cup in her hand. "Sorry."

"Don't be. I'm not." Resting my hip against the counter, I watch the emotions play out across her face. "Don't overthink it, Hailee." I reach out, grasping the hem of her shirt and giving a gentle tug. "I like you, and I'm pretty sure you like me too." When she doesn't say anything, I worry that I've got it all wrong. "But, I mean, I understand if you want to keep this strictly business."

Her shoulders rise and fall as she huffs out a drawn-out sigh. "It's not that I don't want this." Her gaze meets mine, and I can see the fear lingering beneath her lashes. "I made a promise to myself. I can't go through that again." She casts her gaze over the paintings then back to me.

Before I can stop myself, my hands are cupping her face once more. "I would never hurt you." Her eyes search mine, and I hope she can see I'm speaking the truth. "You can trust me."

Chapter Thirteen

Hailee

"You can trust me." The very same words Lila said to me not so long ago, and look where that got me. Broken, alone and on the bones of my ass. After that, I swore I'd never let anyone else take advantage of me. I made a promise to myself to keep my head down and focus on what was important; my art.

But the way Aroha is watching me with hooded eyes has me wanting to go back on my word. The gentle caress of her thumb along my cheek sends shivers of delight through my body, and I can't help but lean into her touch.

"I *want* to trust you," I start.

"But you can't," she finishes. "It's okay, I understand." She slowly draws her hands away with a sad smile. "I'd still like you to paint me… if that's okay?" Her voice has dropped lower, barely more than a whisper. As much as I know I should, I can't deny her that. After all, it's the one thing I *can* give her.

"Of course."

Her eyes light up. "Really?"

The joy shining back at me is more radiant than any sunrise, and impossible to ignore. My lips twitch in the corners, unable to keep from returning her smile. "Yes, really." I wave my arm around the room full of my art. "It's kinda my thing."

She fist pumps the air, bringing her knee up in front of her in a vertical crunch type move. "Yes!"

Her enthusiasm is contagious. I clutch my sides in a fit of giggles as I watch her bouncing around the room. "Anyone would think you'd won the lottery," I manage to say between breaths.

"Oh, but I have!" She grabs hold of my shoulders, leans in and kisses both cheeks. "You've made my day. I can't wait to do this! When can we start?"

The touch of her soft, warm lips on my face is enough to send my mind into a spin. I can tell by the burn in my cheeks that a blush has once again crept onto my face at her closeness. She's staring at me with questioning eyes, and I realise I haven't answered her yet, too distracted by her small act of kindness. One that I know wasn't meant as anything more. Not this time, anyway.

Clearing my throat, I avert my eyes, trying to regain my composure. "Um, it will take some time. I don't have class until tomorrow afternoon, how about first thing in the morning?"

"Tomorrow? Sure! I'll bring breakfast." She grins, reaching out to brush a hair behind my ear. "Thank you."

"You might not be thanking me after you've had to sit for hours on end, holding the same pose. It takes a lot longer to paint than to sketch."

"I don't care if I have to sit for days. I've seen what you can do. It's going to be amazing."

"We'll see." I smile, the unabashed confidence she has in me fills me with pride. For her to see my most personal pieces where I bared my soul, and to understand them, really *feel* what I was going through when I painted them, it's a feeling I will treasure. It's that same feeling I'm hoping to inspire in other artists when I catch my big break.

She places her cup in the sink, turning to me with a sparkle in her eyes. Her fingers trail down my arm lightly before she takes hold of my hand. "It will be. Have more faith in yourself. You've got this." With one final squeeze of my hand, Aroha turns on her heels, breezing past me. "See you in the morning!"

Chapter Fourteen

Aroha

I pull up outside her gate, nervous anticipation swirling in my gut. It's obvious Hailee has been burned before, but if I can just show her that she can trust me, perhaps she'll let us see where this thing between us could go. I know I'm not imagining the connection. She feels it too, I can see it in her eyes when she looks at me. She tries to hide it, but eyes never lie.

Flinging the door open, I step out into the crisp morning air, clasping the bag of freshly baked croissants I'd picked up on the way.

Their enticing scent has my stomach grumbling loudly.

Before I can even knock on the door, it swings open, a bright-eyed Hailee standing before me. *God, she really is gorgeous.*

"Morning." She smiles warmly, ushering me inside.

"Morning! Hope you're hungry." I hold up the bag of goodies before stepping in and out of the cold.

She inhales deeply as I walk past her to the kitchen. "Smells delicious."

"It should be. I got up at the ass-crack of dawn to get these babies fresh out of the oven." Placing the bag on the counter, I begin opening cupboards until I find some plates. Hailee watches with amusement as I make myself at home. "Ta-da! Breakfast of champions," I announce, holding a plate out for her.

"Thanks. The kettle has just boiled. You want a drink?"

"You even have to ask?" I raise an eyebrow, pursing my lips. She laughs and gets to work making our drinks, while I move over to the couch. "I don't think I said yesterday, but, you have a really nice home." I take a bite of my flaky pastry as I take in my surroundings. "It's cosy."

"Isn't that what a home is supposed to be?" She joins me, tucking her feet beneath her legs.

"Yeah, I suppose it is. Where I live, it's more… clinical."

It's her turn to quirk a brow at me this time. "Clinical?"

"Yeah. Like, it doesn't feel lived in. Not like this." I gesture around the room. "This place has character."

"Do you not spend much time at home then?"

"Mm, no, I do. I just spend most of my time in my room. I live with a really uptight dude who likes everything in its place. Everything is in shades of black and white, and always top-of-the-line stuff. He'd never dream of having miss-matched furniture." I chuckle, holding my hand to the side of my mouth as if divulging some big secret. "He'd shit a brick if he stepped foot in my room. I need colour in my life."

"You live together, and he's never seen your room? Not even in passing?"

"Nah, he keeps to himself. As long as I don't mess up his space, he doesn't care what I do in mine. I just don't think he could handle the rainbow vibe I've got going on." I grin, knowing she of all people can understand the need for colour.

"Nothing wrong with a bit of rainbow." She strokes the multi-coloured blanket thrown over the arm of the couch.

We settle into a comfortable silence while we finish eating, and then I collect the plates and take them to the sink to rinse.

"Don't worry about those. I can do them later." She waves me away from the counter, leading me through to the next room, which appears to be her bedroom come studio.

On the floor in the centre of the room is a mattress with a drop cloth covering it. There is an easel set up near the foot of the bed with a palette of paints ready and waiting. To the left of the mattress is the wicker chair from her entranceway, also covered in a dark drop cloth.

"I wasn't sure how you wanted to do this so I prepared for a few scenarios." She pulls an oversized shirt over her singlet and jeans. It has a rainbow of colours splattered on it from the last time she painted. "You can use the mattress or the chair, or even stand if you like, though I wouldn't recommend it." She laughs. "Your feet will be killing you by the end of the day."

"I'm fine with the mattress. More cushion for my ass." I grin back at her, kicking my shoes off by the door. "Where can I put my clothes?"

"W-what?" She looks at me in confusion and it dawns on me, she thought I meant a clothed portrait.

"Oh, I thought… I was hoping you could do one of *just me*."

Chapter Fifteen

Hailee

"Oh." No other words will come out as I stand here gaping at her. I guess I should have known that was what she meant when she asked me to paint her. She *is* a nude model after all.

"Is that okay?"

"Um, yeah." I shake my head with a laugh. "Sorry, that's fine. You can change in the bathroom, through there." I point down the hall to the only other room in the house. "There's a robe hanging on the back of the door if you want to wear it." She nods and brushes past me, eliciting a shiver down my spine. Her musky perfume lingers and I find myself sucking in a deep breath, desperate to take it all in.

God, what have I gotten myself into? She's a temptation I never bargained for when I signed up for this class, one that I'm not sure I'm strong enough to deny. I'm not even sure I *want* to anymore either. Her energy and enthusiasm is so uplifting, something I feel has been missing in my life of late.

I try to occupy myself with setting the room up some more, but my mind keeps wandering. A part of me wants to march over there, throw open the door and take her in my arms, but a voice in my head keeps telling me no. This is business. Nothing more, nothing less.

When she steps into the room wearing only my robe, my heart skips a beat, and my throat dries up. The thought of her bare, coffee-coloured skin underneath *my* robe, the robe I wear every morning, is driving me to distraction. She is utterly breath-taking.

Her ebony hair hangs loose over her shoulder, framing her face in a waterfall of silk. I almost want to reach out and stroke it, but I stop myself.

Her fingers fumble with the tie around her waist, slowly undoing it until the robe falls open and I get a glimpse at just a little more. When she shrugs her shoulders, the robe cascades down her back, to the floor, leaving her exposed.

Her eyes never leave mine as she steps onto the mattress, lowering to a seated position, her back angled toward me so I can see the beautiful artwork she carries with her everywhere she goes. Swirls of ink cover her back and the top of her thigh, paying tribute to her heritage.

"Beautiful," I whisper as I my eyes follow the trail of ink across her body. "Did it hurt?"

"Mm, some of it. It's a good kind of pain though. It's more bearable when you know something good will come out of it." Her eyes meet mine and I know what she's thinking. Through my own pain, I created something beautiful too. And she's right. Those paintings are some of my favourite pieces. I hadn't intended for them to be seen by anyone else, but perhaps if I put them on display, it could be a form of closure for me. A way to really say goodbye to my past and prove that I'm okay.

I smile and nod my head, tucking my chin into my chest while I toy with the brush in my hand. "Something good definitely came out of it." I peek up at her again. "They're gorgeous." Tucking a hair behind my ear, I whisper, *"You're* gorgeous." I swallow the lump in my throat, averting my eyes as I try to calm my erratic heart. It's impossible to stay on track when she's looking at me like that. What is it about her that makes me want to go against everything I've worked hard to be?

I move back to my safe place, behind my easel, and catch a glimpse of her smile as she turns her head away. Seeing how those two simple words have affected her is enough to send a rush of heat through me.

Focus, Hailee.

"Is this position okay? I thought it would be cool to have my ink up on the wall." She cranes her neck around to face me before turning back towards the window. The sun chooses this exact moment to peek out from behind the clouds, casting a beacon of light across her.

I suck in a sharp breath. "Don't move." Relaxing my eyes, I hone in on the halo of light around her head, giving her an almost angelic look. Dabbing my brush in the paint, I begin.

Chapter Sixteen

Aroha

There's a method to my madness. I want her to feel safe and comfortable with me, not like I'm a cougar on the prowl. When I was watching her sketch me yesterday, her eyes kept following the lines of my ink, so I knew she was intrigued by them. Turning my back on her not only gives her the sense that I'm taking this as seriously as she is, but also gives her a front row seat to the markings that captivate her.

I'm used to having people watch me, but for very different reasons. They see my tatts and the colour of my skin, and whether they say it out loud or not, I can see they've already labelled me; just another Maori to keep an eye on. I see them pretending to be busy while following me with their eyes, making sure I'm not trying to get a bit of five-finger discount. Really, they have nothing to worry about with me. I'm as honest as the day is long. Too honest, some might say. I'm not afraid to call a spade a spade, and if you try to tell me otherwise, I'll damn well call you out on it. It's just how I was raised.

My father is Maori, and my mother, a blonde-haired, blue-eyed Pakeha. Ebony and ivory. That's how I got my mocha skin and green eyes. I pay homage to my roots through my tattoos, linking my past to my future through design. But that's not what most people see when they look at me.

Except for Hailee. She doesn't look at me the way others do, like I'm someone to be wary of. No. She sees something different. She sees me.

I know she was uncomfortable about me seeing her paintings. It was obvious how much pain she'd been in when she did them. I've never really understood art before, or perhaps I've never taken the time to really look, but as soon as my eyes landed on those ones stacked in the corner, I knew they were special.

Showing her the art on my skin is my way of showing her that pain can sometimes lead to good things, even if you can't feel that at the time. Hopefully, it will also show her that she can trust me, as I'm putting my trust in her.

After a few hours of sitting in the quiet, save for the stroke of brush on canvas, Hailee lets out a tiny groan. A quick glance over my shoulder shows me she is leaning back, her hands on her lower back as she stretches.

"You must be getting sick of sitting in one position. Do you want to take a break?" She steps out from behind her easel, brushing her hands down her shirt front. There is a smudge of paint on the tip of her nose, and fresh streaks of colour line her shirt. But, it's her eyes that take my breath away. They almost sparkle with contentment. It must be such a nice feeling, to have something you do make you so happy.

I nod. Clasping my hands together, I push them up towards the ceiling, doing my own stretches, before pulling myself up to my feet. She doesn't bat an eye as I turn to face her in all my naked glory.

I can't help but grin as I notice even more paint on her face, and even some in her hair. "I thought the paint was meant to go on the canvas." Reaching out, I swipe a finger through the blob along her jaw, pulling it back to show her. She giggles and I can't help myself, I run my paint-covered finger down her nose.

She grins at me, taking a swipe of her own and brushing it across my cheek.

"Oh, it's like that, is it?" I grab the palette from its perch on top of the easel and using two fingers, I scoop up a big blob, holding it out with a glint in my eye.

"No." She shakes her head, but the laughter in her eyes spurs me on. "You wouldn't."

"Wouldn't I?" I lunge forward, smearing it down her cheek and neck.

"Two can play at that game." Slapping her hand down on the palette, she charges towards me, paint dripping from her hand and onto the floor. I squeal and dart out of her reach.

"You'll have to catch me first." I jump onto the mattress, my stance wide, ready to pounce. I quickly dip my fingers in the paint, tossing the palette to the floor so I have both arms at my disposal. "Come at me." I beckon her with a crook of my finger.

She leaps onto the mattress, quicker than I was anticipating, and we tumble down in a heap, giggling and fending each other off. With paint all over our hands, we wrestle, each trying to hold the other's arms at bay. I lose my grip, my hand sliding down her arm as it comes down to meet my bare chest.

We both stop, my chest heaving beneath her hand as it slips down toward my neck. Our eyes meet, and suddenly the laughter is replaced with a heated stare. I lick my lips, and bring my hand up to hers. With shaking fingers, I take hold, bringing it lower, until she is cupping the swell of my breast. I don't miss the sharp inhale she takes as her hand closes around me, gently kneading.

I arch my back, pushing against her hand with a soft moan. She pulls her lip in between her teeth, her eyes flicking down to my lips and back up to my eyes.

Trailing my hand back up her arm to her neck, I let my fingers thread through her hair, softly coaxing her to shift closer. With her breath mingling with mine, I take my chance, tilting my head up to brush my lips against hers.

Chapter Seventeen

Hailee

Her lips are just as soft as I imagined they'd be, and when she pulls away, I whimper, not wanting to give them up.

A smile graces those perfect lips of hers as she stares up at me, her grip on my hair, firm. Now that I've had a taste of her, I can't get myself to pull away. The voice inside my head telling me to be professional is pushed to the back where I can no longer hear it.

My fingers keep working her soft flesh, and I can feel her heart pounding beneath my hand as I dip my head to meet her lips again. Her tongue darts out, lapping at my lips, seeking entry, and when I open up for her, she moans into my mouth, sending an inferno of heat straight to my core.

Her free hand travels down my body until it lands firmly on my ass, pulling me closer to her. Our legs entwine, and I bring my knee up to press against the warmth between her thighs as she rocks back and forth.

Releasing my hair, she brings her hand down to join the other, pushing up under my top. Gripping the edges, she lifts and I pull back just enough to allow the material to pass before pressing against her again. Just the feel of her silky skin on mine has me desperate for more. I roll onto my back, and she follows, straddling my hips as she peppers kisses along my neck and down to my breasts. I arch my back, needing to feel her lips on me, but she pulls away with a grin.

"I think maybe we need to take this to the bathroom." She nods her head towards my chest. With a confused expression, I peer down at my body and then back to hers. The corners of my lips pull up as I giggle. We look like some kind of Picasso painting, with smears of colour all over us. There is a black hand print on her neck with a smudge leading down to her breast. My arm and neck are now a lovely shade of blue mixed with green.

"I think you might be right." I push up onto my elbows, not yet ready to move. With her body so close to mine, I can get a better look at the tattoo that starts above her breast. It starts as a small koru opening into a heart, which is also the base of a bigger koru weaving under her arm and over her neck. It's truly beautiful.

Tentatively, I reach out, trailing a finger along the design, feeling the skin raised slightly where the ink has been pushed in.

My soft touch has her skin pebbling and her nipples tightening before my eyes. I trace the ink, slowly circling lower. She closes her eyes, tipping her head back as she begins to rock her hips against me. I want so much to pull one of those tight buds into my mouth, to hear her screaming my name as she comes undone.

I've opened Pandora's Box and there's no going back now. Everything I thought I needed pales in comparison to how much I need her right now.

"I need you," I whisper huskily, letting my hands weave up to cup her face. "Please."

Chapter Eighteen

Aroha

"I need you."
The words are like music to my ears, and I feel the same way. I need her like I need air. She's so much more than I could've imagined. She's everything.

Staring down at her face full of love and light, all I want to do is make her happy. I want to taste her, touch her, bring her to her knees.

Brushing my lips against hers in a soft embrace, I try to convey all my emotions. Everything I am feeling in this moment.

"I need you too."

Her smile is something songs are written about as she beams up at me. "Bathroom?" she says with a glint in her eye.

Just you try and stop me.

"I'll wash your back if you wash mine."

"Deal." She presses her lips to mine with a sigh of pleasure.

Before we get too carried away again, I push back, climbing off her lap and offering a hand to help her up. Without a word, I lead her through to her own bathroom.

I turn the mixer to warm before closing the door and facing the beautiful girl before me. Even with paint through her hair and all up her body, she's still the most stunning creature I've ever laid eyes on.

With a crook of my finger, I beckon her to me. Dropping to my knees, I reach out and take hold of the waistband of her jeans, slowly edging them down her long alabaster legs. Her white cotton panties come down next. I lean forward, planting a kiss atop the light-coloured curls.

Her hands thread through my hair, tugging until I stand, our bodies merely a breath away from each other.

Stepping into the shower, I grab a washcloth and lather it in soap. I push her up against the wall. Bringing her hands above her head, I hold them in place with one hand, while I lazily trail the cloth across her body. I start with her neck, and as the cloth moves lower, so too do my lips.

She squirms beneath my touch, arching her back and pressing her breasts into me. I once again drop to my knees, licking a trail down to the apex of her thighs. I run my hand down the back of her leg, lifting it over my shoulder, opening her up for me.

My hands roam back to her ass, pulling her in nice and close before my tongue darts out and I lick from opening to clit in one motion. Her hips buck and she moans low and sweet, "Oh yeah."

With my mouth secured on her clit, I plunge two fingers between her folds and she sucks in a sharp breath. "Yes!" Spurred on by her cries, I thrust my fingers in and out, my hand squeezing her ass and holding her against me while my tongue flicks her clit relentlessly.

Her fingers tangle in my hair, as she rocks her pussy into my face, riding towards her release. She's so wound up it doesn't take long before she throws her head back, crying out, "Aroha! God, yes!"

I soften my tongue, lapping up every last drop as she comes down from her high. With her head resting against the wall and one arm thrown across her face, she fumbles to find my chin, bringing me up to meet her.

"Hi," I say with a grin, planting a kiss on her lips so she can taste herself.

"Hi, yourself." She drops her arms around my neck. "That was… wow. You're *really* good at that."

"What can I say? My mother always told me to treat people the way you want to be treated." I grin up at her with a wink.

"Is that right?" I nod and she chuckles. "Well, I guess I'd better get to work then."

Blank Canvas

Chapter Nineteen

Hailee

I step around her, pressing kisses along her shoulder and following the ink with my tongue. My arms slip around her waist, pulling her back against my breasts as I continue to worship her body with my lips.

Her tattoos give me a pattern to follow as I make my way down her body. I land on my knees, her ripe ass in line with my face. The ink swirls across her skin here too, dipping in and coming to a stop where her thighs meet.

I run my hands over her silky skin, my thumbs brushing along her inner thighs eliciting a moan from her as she pushes further into the wall. Her hips tilt up, giving me better access to her.

Using my tongue, I show my admiration for the work of art on display before me. My hands move around to cup her breasts as my tongue moves closer to her centre, lapping at every piece of skin I can. A shudder runs through her body as I circle around her folds, finding her clit. Teasing her with my tongue, I'm careful to use the lightest of touches. I want to make this last.

"Hailee, please." Her voice is hoarse with desire and it thrills me to know I'm the reason.

Increasing the pressure of my tongue, I slip a finger inside her, rubbing the soft walls within. When she starts to rock her hips, I add another, hooking it round to find the ridged area I know is there.

"Fuck!" Her hips buck wildly and I know I've found what I'm looking for. I latch my lips around her clit, sucking in time with my fingers as I tweak her nipple.

"Shit! Fuck! I'm gonna come!"

I hum against her clit, urging her over the edge. Her hands slap on the tiled walls as her pussy grinds into my face, chasing her release.

Her body seizes as she comes undone. I grip her hips and bury my face between her thighs, my tongue delving deep to lap up all her juices.

When her breathing slows and she can speak again, she cranes her neck to look back at me over her shoulder with a grin.

"Now *that* is how you treat a lady."

Chapter Twenty

Aroha

With a towel wrapped firmly around me, and another drying my hair, I pad back to the bedroom where Hailee is already behind her easel. She's wearing the same paint-stained shirt and nothing else. Her eyes crinkle in the corners and she purses her lips as she scrutinises her morning's work.

"What's the verdict?" I ask, coming to stand beside her. I reach out to tuck a strand of hair behind her ear before turning my eyes to the painting. "Oh my God." The words are barely more than a whisper as the towel falls from my hands and I cover my mouth.

"You like it?" she asks with concern. Her fingers fumble with the brush in her hand, something I know she does when she's nervous.

I shake my head. "No. I don't like it."

"Oh—"

I place my hand on hers, pinning her with my gaze. "I *love* it."

"Really?"

"Really." I turn back to the painting. "It's beautiful."

"Well, I had a pretty stunning muse." She nudges me with her elbow and I can't help the grin that spreads across my face. "Of course, it's not quite finished yet..." She lets her voice trail off, her eyes roving down my towelled body.

"I guess break time is over then, huh?" Spinning on my heel, I drop the towel and strut to the mattress where it all began.

"Mm, I think I need to get another close look at those tattoos though. You know, for research." She grins as she stalks towards me, discarding her shirt. Sitting behind me, her legs wrapped around my waist, she plants a kiss on the back of my neck. "Thank you," she whispers, nuzzling her head in my hair.

I peek over my shoulder at her, confused. "What for?"

"For sharing this with me. For letting me see that once you get past the pain, you can create something amazing."

I turn, bringing my hands up to cradle her face. "You didn't need me to show you that. You were already on your way to seeing it, you just needed to let yourself." I poke a finger at her forehead. "You need to get out of your head sometimes and just see things for what they are. The hurt you were holding onto, it doesn't define who you are, what you do with that hurt does. And, baby?" I brush my lips against hers. "What you do is pure magic."

Chapter Twenty-One

Hailee

The door opens and Aroha steps out onto the platform wearing her robe. Angelique bustles to the front of the room, instructing us all to tear off our pages and prepare our canvases. Over her shoulder, I can see Aroha making a beeline for the chaise lounge, a tiny smile on her face, no doubt remembering the dream I'd told her about.

"Remember, if you prefer, you can sketch a rough outline first and add paint after, it really is up to you." Angelique holds up a cloth.

"Don't forget to keep your brush clean between colours. It's always handy to have a cloth within reach to dry the brush between as well." She swivels to look at Aroha. "Whenever you're ready."

Aroha nods and takes a deep breath, her eyes finding mine in the crowd. With a smile, she shrugs her shoulders, letting the robe fall to the floor before lying across the chaise on her side with her back to the room. She braces herself on an elbow, and turns her head to look over her shoulder, once again meeting my gaze.

I lick my lips as I recall the way her skin felt under my tongue only a matter of hours ago. I spent so much time taking in her every curve, I'm sure I could paint her with my eyes closed, but I don't.

I stare at the blank canvas before me, envisaging what it will become. The possibilities are endless. With a splash of colour, it can be anything I want it to be. And as I turn my gaze to the beauty who has stolen my heart and helped me find my light again, I know that whatever I do, it will be so much more with her by my side, than it would be without.

I smile, a secret smile just for her.

Picking up my brush, I dab it in a bit of colour and begin.

The End

Blank Canvas

A note from Cyan

Thank you so much to all the readers and bloggers out there for taking the time to read Blank Canvas! I hope you enjoyed reading it as much as I enjoyed writing it. Without you, I wouldn't be able to keep doing what I love, and then I'd just be a crazy lady with voices in my head, and we don't want that!

I'd like to take a moment to thank fellow kiwi and author, Nicole Goodin. Not only is she a great friend, she's also my sounding board. We bounce ideas off each other, sharing our covers and teasers before anyone else sees them. It certainly makes this whole writing business a lot easier to navigate when you have someone on your side who understands! So, Nicole, thanks a bunch!

Thank you also to my amazingly talented friend, Trina. Without her, I'm sure I would say something silly and get myself into all sorts of trouble. She has been with me since the very beginning, cheering me on and casting her eagle eyes over my words to catch any errors before they go to print.

To the Ink Slinging Sisters, thank you for all your support and encouragement! I love each and every one of you and hope to one day meet you all and squish you in a big bear hug!

Theresa, yes, I'm talking to you, your unwavering support and kind words have been amazing. Thank you so much for being my friend.

Cyan's links

Cyan Tayse is the pen name of a multi-genre author based in New Zealand. After a lot of coaxing from friends, she decided to embark on a journey of discovery. Yes, that's right, she discovered her inner smut, and brought it to life in her debut novella, Have you Ever...?

Cyan can often be found lurking on social media, and she loves to hear from fellow authors and readers.

http://www.cyantayse.weebly.com
https://www.facebook.com/CyanTayse
https://www.instagram.com/cyantayse
https://www.Twitter.com/cyan_tayse